THE UNFORGIVEN CRUSH

ELARA QUINN

CONTENTS

Chapter 1

I woke up to the sun in my eyes and the birds singing their morning songs. I heard swift footsteps run pass my door and low wishpers. I slowly creeped up to my door and turned the knob. I held my breathe and busted the door open.

"Boooo!!!"

My siblings feel to the floor in shock. I was laughing so hard tears were forming in my eyes."Sissy you scared me and bubba! That not fuwy!" I looked at Skylar and Ryder with their arms folded and lips pouted. I picked up Ryder and kissed his cheek.

"I'm sorry Ryder Sissy didn't mean to scare you!"

Skylar wrapped her arms around my leg squeezing the hell out of it.

"You too Sky!" I picked up Sky and walked downstairs.

Mother was cooking eggs, grits and bacon, which is my personal favorite.

"Mommy, mommy sissy scared me!" Ryder said jumping out of my arms. I chuckled while shaking my head. I sat Skylar down and kissed dad on the cheek."Morning dad!""Morning sweetpea!" Dad fixed his glasses and flipped the newspaper over to read the front headline.

"These damn werewolf hunters killing our kind!" Said dad with a slight anger tone.

Mom laid down a cup of coffee for dad, milk for Ryder and Sky, and orange juice for me.

"Valen you better get going to training or you will be late!" I looked at the clock. The time was 7:45. Mom was right! I grabbed my backpack while slipping on my shoes.

Rushing, I opened the door, not paying attention to anything or anyone, I bumped into a hard constructive chest. Two large hands pushed back my small body followed by a deep sexy voice.

"Are you alright?"

I looked up to see Rondni. He is one of my dads oldest friends. Rondni is 35 and my dad is 37. I instantly jumped in his arms and yelled his name. "Rondni!" He spun me around like a little girl and I giggled like a five year old. Dad, mom, and the twins came to see Rondni at the door.

"Sup Rondni! How's it been?" Said my dad while doing the little man handshake with Rondni. Mother hugged him and asked how work treated him. Of course he replied qith 'just fine'. Ryder and Skylar squeezed the mess out of his legs.

I remembered that I was running late for training and needed to leave.

"I gotta go for training so don't leave to early." I said sprinting out the front door.

After practice I came home hearing laughter coming from inside the dining room. I walked around the corner and my family and Rondni were all playing a game and kackaling.

"Hey sweetpea. How was training?" My dad asked

I leaned on the wall and sighed. "I feel like passing out!" Dad chuckled at me while I smiled.

"Well go wash up dinner is almost ready." I nodded at dad and ran up the stairs to my room.

45 minutes later I walked in the dining room with mom setting plates down and dad and Rondni in a deep conversation.

"So how long are you planning on staying!" I asked taking the seat next to Rondni.

He looked at dad with a nervous look on his face.

"I'm on a business trip and since I haven't seen you guys for a while I thought I could stay here for a couple of weeks. Also I know someone is turning 18 in a week!"

My eyes widened when he mentioned my birthday I felt blessed for him to remember that. My dad looked at Rondni real stern like he getting on to a child.

"Well, Rondni I think me and Carol don't.... care! Stay for as long as you need!!"

A couple of days have passed my birthday is only 3 days away. I got out of bed and started my shower. I was already stripped down to my underwear and bra when I seen that my towel rack was empty. I mind-linked my mom.

Mom I am out of towels can you bring me one. Please!

Sorry honey I'm a little busy right now with your father. No one else is awake just go get it.

Ewww...! But I'm basicly naked!

Your dad won't let me leave!

Ugh.... fine!

I looked out my bedroom door cautiously, to make sure no one was really up. I walked down stairs, still making sure no one was up. Once I seen no one I walked to the laundry room humming. I opened the door to a shirtless Rondni messing with the dryer.

"Rondni!" I said shocked.

He looked me up and down. My heart had stopped. RONDNI WAS SEEING ME ALMOST NAKED!!!

"I... I just came to get a um... a towel! I didn't know you were in here. So..sorry!" I said nervously

I tripped on a pile of clothes and fell on Rondni. His large hands held my waist. I was basically straddling him with my hands on his chest. I looked into his ocean blue eyes. His jet black hair was ruffled, but still looked good. He had a perfect jaw line. His muscular arms and his abs. I was brought back when Rondni spoke to me.

"You okay Valen?"

My name rolled off his tongue so perfectly. Like it was meant for him to say it.

" Y...yeah what about you!?"

He sat up and I got off of him.

"Here... you need this!"

I looked at him confused. Why would I need his t-shirt.

"Your not appropriately dressed!" He said pointing and looking away from me. My face was steaming. I quickly threw the t-shirt on and grabbed my towel running back to my room.

The rest of the day I couldn't get what happened this morning out of my head. Mom called for us at the dinner table. She had my favorite; steak, mashed potatoes, grilled non-cut green beans, salad, and a chocolate lava cake. Dad was pouring mom and Rondni a glass of wine. While I was stuck with water. He goes on about how I'm to young to drink. Werewolves don't get drunk!

"Can I have everyone's attention." Dad stood up at the table like he was at a gala or something when they give those big speeches.

"Valen, I just want to say that life is tough and your going to go through some hardships, but who ever your mate is I hope he treats you right and that you can always lean on him when you need to. My first child is finally turning 18. Soon you will be leaving to go and live with your special someone. I just wanted to let you know that I love you no matter what happens because your my sweetpea and always will be! So live life to the fullest and learn from your mistakes, be who you wanna be!"

Dad sat down and mom was crying. Ryder and Sky were blinking, confused of what my dad was going on about. I stood up and hugged both my parents.

"I love you guys so much! I couldn't ask for any better parents then you guys!" I said pulling them as tight as I can.

After dinner Dad and Mom went out while Ryder and Sky was at our neighbor's house playing with their kids. I was laying on the couch in my pjs. I was just minding my own business flipping through the channels when the remote was snatched out my hand.

"Hey! I was using that" I said with a little sass.

Rondni walked around and stood in front of the T.V. He waved the remote in my face mocking me.

"Come get it if you want it so bad!"

I scuffed and just rolled my eyes.

"I guess you weren't into that episode then!"

He walked away i jumped up on his back trying to reach the remote.

"Come on Rondni I was watching that!"

He was just laughing at me. This was not funny! He fell back into the couch squishing me.

"Hows the oxygen levels under there!"

I was trying to gulp down some air.

"Your suffocating me! GET OFF!"

Rondni sat up and I took the advantage to push him down, but as always my plans don't work. Instead of him on the floor with me standing on top of him in victory I was on the floor with him hovering over me in triumph.

"I guess I get to watch what I want to watch then. Sucks being the loser doesn't it."

I rolled my eyes and smirked.

"At least I have all the guys to hold my attention! Who could turn down this body of a goddess!" His eyes were turning from black to blue. I pushed myself away and looked at Rondni.

"I.. I'm going to bed!" And with that said he walked up to the guest room. I felt like I did or said something wrong. Like I have upset him.

CHAPTER 2

Today is my birthday!! I finally turn 18 at exactly 12 AM. Which is in 2 hours. I tried to beg my mom to let me have my party at 12, but no... it was too late.

I was scrolling through Netflix to find a movie. Cause I was bored out of my mind. When a werewolf turns of age they don't only find their mates they also can start transformation into their wolf if they didn't have premature transformation.

I started feeling a little uncomfortable in my bed so I just walked around my room looking through all the stuff I had. I have a lot of stuff. I've went through so much stuff that I was starting to think I was a horder.

About an hour passed and it was getting really hot in my room and I was booty shorts and a tank top. My vision was getting blurry and the room was spinning. I stumbled to my door and I was in exscrusiating pain. I fell to the floor screaming.

After I fell to the floor footsteps flooded my hearing. Rondni was beside me calling my name. Mom and Dad were not to far behind him. Everything was blurry I could see dad telling Rondni to carry me. I felt pain engulfing me.

We were outside and I was laying on the grass trying to calm down. The pain died down for a moment and I felt every bone in my body snap in two and reshape themselves. I opened my eyes to see mom, dad, and Rondni looking at me. I was much taller than them.

"How are you feeling honey!" Mom asked me.

I went to say something, but the only thing that left my mouth was a grunt. I realized I have to use mind-link.

I'm okay just a little shaken up

I looked at my paws they were grey and huge. My mom took out her phone and took a picture of me. She showed me what I looked like.

I was light grey ,almost white, with deep green golden eyes. I shook my fur and it felt good to be in this form.

The moon sat high in the sky at the dead center meaning it was 12 a.m.I am officially 18!

I walked behind a tree and shifted back. Mom handed me some clothes and made sure I was okay. The wind blew in the night air. The smell is amazing!! I love the smell of pine, grass, flowers, and rain water. Inbetween all of those I smelt something memorizing. The smell hit my nostrils.

It smelt like a sweet honey suckle on a spring day and salty sea water on a misty morning. My mom snapped her fingers at me because I wasn't paying her any attention. Rondni and Dad were waiting for us in the yard. We walked towards them when I seen were the smell was coming from. One word screamed in my head. MATE!!

We all went to bed afterwards, but I couldn't go to sleep. It was 4 in the morning and I was wide awake. I heard someone downstairs and I decided to investigate. I mean why not? I can't sleep anyways! I quietly made my way out the door when his scent hit me in my face. If I knew he was in there then he knows to.

I made my way down the stairs. I walked to the kitchen. He picked up his cup of whiskey and wolfsbane, if you drink wolfsbane then you can get drunk, he finished the cup and sat it down on the counter.

"What is it Valen?"

I jumped at his tone. I shyly stood behind him reaching to touch his back, but quickly retreated.

"I just heard commotion and I just came to see who it was. Plus I can't sleep."

He poured more in his cup and sat the bottle down making a clank. He went to lift it up to drink it, but I pushed his arm down from his face.

"Why are you drinking in the first place?" I asked looking into his ocean blue eyes.

He slowly places the cup down and turned towards me. I didn't realize he was only wearing sweatpants with his American Eagle underwear showing at his hips. I couldn't say much for myself. I was wearing a large t-shirt and panties.

"I just am!" He sighed and pinched his nose.

"But why? I don't think you are just drinking to drink! Especially with wolfsbane in it!"

I stepped forward, now being an inch apart. He looked at my eyes then my lips. He sat back on the counter and sighed. Man what is up with this man sighing.

"Because Valen, no 18 year old girl wants a 35 year old man as a mate. And I'm assuming that you came down here to reject me because I'm not what you were expecting."

This big man was gonna make little ole me cry. What made him think that. I opened my mouth, but no words escaped. I know how I felt, but he didn't. I placed my hands on the side of his face and pulled him into a kiss. He was shocked, but he gradually leaned into it. He wrapped his hands on my legs. I wrap them around his waist while my hands were tangled in his hair. My wolf Celia was jumping up and down in my head. She was pretty excited. Rondni sat me on the island and parted for a minute. I whimpered, but I needed some oxygen. I huffed and then smiled.

"Does that answer your question!"

He looked up at me with a smirk plastered on his face. He picked me up and walked to the livingroom. He threw me on the couch. He pulled my shirt off exposing my bare chest. He stopped and looked at me. I wasn't ready for sex, but I wanted him to mark me.

"I'm not ready yet, but I do want you to mark me."

His eyes grew dark and he lowered his head and whispered in my ear.

"With pleasure!"

He kissed my lips softly, then it became deeper. He swiped his tongue on my bottom lip and I granted him access. He slowly made his way down my jawline, halfway down my neck til he found my sweet spot. I bite my lip trying not to moan. He licked it and I couldn't hold it in anymore. He let out a low seductive growl. I felt his kanines brush against my skin, when the lights in the livingroom came on and a womans voice filled my ears.

"Rondni who is this?" My mom asked.

I hide my face when she walked over.

"Oh dear! I'm so sorry for interrupting."

Rondni sat up leaving my face bare. I am so going to kill him for this.

"Valen!" My mom screamed. I covered my chest. When I heard dad come running down the steps.

"What's wrong hon..." My face was as red as a tomato. I was caught by my parents. Well that was great. As my dad went to screaming at me a beeping sound was now his voice. I open my eyes to only realize I was dreaming.

I swing my legs out of bed and head down to the kitchen. Rondni's scent was faded threw out the house. He had already left for work. What am I going to do. Dad would never approve. Mom doesn't care. What would he say. What if he rejects me.He is not going to reject us Valen. How do you know Cecilia?Why would he we're beautiful. Your all kinds of things.I love my wolf she just knows how to lift my spirit. No one was really home so I went to my special place. The meadow is secretly hidden by the trees and other shrubs. A small waterfall makes it seem like I am the only person in the world.

I walk to the water and glance at myself in my wolf form. This place is so relaxingI know. I come here often to just let the world take me. I couldn't dream of a better place.Let's go for a swim. Our fur needs a little shining.I immediately jump in. The crisp cool water soaks my fur. The sun glistens on the water when a different shadow hovers over me.Having fun!Rondni I thought you were at work. How... did you...?I had a little hunch.I knew exactly what he was talking about. There is no hiding it. It was totally obvious.Look stop beating around the bush and just reject me.Is what I wanted to say, but I couldn't think straight. My mind was all over the place. Rondni walked behind a tree and shifted."Aren't you going to shift back!"I shook my head. I forgot clothes out of all things I could bring, I didn't have clothes.

I didn't bring clothes to change back into."Here, take this!"I look up and see a shirtless Rondni. Aww... he gave me his shirt. Look at that bodyCecila! Get it together!Sorry, but just look at him!I took the shirt from Rondni and shifted behind some trees. I stood there. I was so nervous. what could possibly happen?

We both sit in the grass starring into the sky. Nothing said. Not a thing was happening.

I sit up and look at the waterfall hit the lake. It is always the most beautiful place.

"Hey Ron can I tell you something?!"

"Yeah what's up?"

"One day I want to get married here in this spot. My favorite spot!"

"I'll keep that noted!"

We both shift back and head back home.

CHAPTER 3

"Katy help me!"

"Help you with what exactly! It's... totally obvious!"

Thud

"Did you really have to throw me down Valen."

I smiled and gave Katy a hand. She has been my best-friend through thick and thin. We are training partners since no one else is as good as us. Not bragging. Oh what am I saying I am bragging.

"What about our one year vacation. What are you going to do since you now have that special someone."

She took a sip of her water. I was really scratching my head at that one.

"I don't know Katy I'm so confused on what's going on. I haven't even spoke to him in 2 days, and it feels like an eternity!"

Katy chuckled. We both walked out of the training area.

"I don't know why you are asking me I haven't found my mate yet. Yours is a plus, his older meaning he's had a lot more experience!" She wiggled her eyebrows at me. This girl is always in the gutter.

"I'm home!" Me and Katy dropped our things at her door. It was very quiet in her house. The very opposite from mine."MOM! DAD! AARON! I guess no one is home, that's not suprising." I chuckled. This child is so bipolar. She hates her families company, but can't stand it when they are not here."Pizza and Netflix?" "Your a guiness Valen! I'll call it in pepperoni and meatlovers!""Yes of course!"She went to the kitchen to find the number, my phone vibrates in my pocket

Mom- Hey! I'm assuming u are at Katy's. Me and ur Father are going out tonight. Don't come home late. Babysitter has the munchkins. <3 love ya.

Me-ok! Love ya too!!

We watched Stranger Things. That is my favorite on Netflix. I helped Katy clean up our pizza and popcorn disaster, and walked home. I only live 2 blocks away from Katy.

I open the door and it was completely dark inside. It was 2 in the morning kind of explains why. Everyone is asleep. I creeped around and made my way into the kitchen. I was making myself a glass of water when I felt his hands wrap around my waist. I felt chills run down my spine. I could feel his breathe on my neck. His smell overwhelmed me.

"Where were you!?" His voice was low and deep. I was scrambling words in my head to give him a clear answer.

"I... I was at Katy's!" He grabbed my glass and sat it on the counter top. My wolf was screaming in my head. She was starting to give me a headache.

"Are you Rondni or Maxin!" I knew that this was not Rondni. He stepped back and turned the lights on. "Valen when did you get back home?" I chuckled. He doesn't remember.

"I just got home Rondni, were you trying to get laid tonight!?" His eyes got wide. He started walking towards me. I was now pushed up against the fridge. He smashed his lips into mine.

I have to stop daydreaming. I must be having withdraw als.Sadly none of that happened. He wasn't even home. I made my way to my room just lying in bed. I need to tell him that I want him.

Thank God it's the weekend. I woke up feeling cold. I open my eyes and stretched. I had nothing on. Where were my clothes. They were all on the floor damp from sweat. What was I dreaming last night. I went through my dresser looking for something decent. I heard footsteps coming up the stairs. Please don't come in! Please don't come in!

Just as I was wishing no one would bust through my door Rondni comes in with out a knock.

"Hey Valen you wanna get...!"

"Get out Rondni!" I was running to my bedsheets trying to cover my exposed body.

"Jesus you could have closed your eyes!"He smirked and shook his head. He came and sat on my bed with me tangled in the sheets, still naked!

"I was asking if you wanted to go and get some breakfast somewhere in town, before your siblings come home?"

He wants to spend time with me. He is so sweet! God he is a freaking god. I can feel my face heating up.

"Do you or are you distracted!?" He cupped my face with his hand. Please kiss me.

"Get dressed. I'll be downstairs."Ugh..... Why!?

I got up did my morning routine. I put on some black ripped jeans and a white long sleeve crop top. I walked downstairs to see him paitenly waiting for me. We walked out and made our way to the restaurant.

Denny Diner and Breakfast is my absolute favorite breakfast place ever. When I was younger when Mom had work Dad and Rondni would bring me to Denny's on their day off. I always got the same thing the hash brown bowl with eggs and bacon. He opened the car door for me. "My lady!" I giggled. Him and Dad would race to open the door for them to let me out. Rondni would always win!

"It's been a minute since we've been here!" He laughed slowly remembering the old days.

"Yes it really has! Last time we ate here was when I told you I was leaving. That day was hard.." I remember that day like it was yesterday."

When I was 13 Rondni picked me up early from training. I thought it was just an ordinary day.

"Hey, wanna go to Denny's?" I hopped into Rondni's convertible excitedly. I love Denny's."What's the occasion Ron?! Normally dad is with you." I asked as he smiled kind of sad like. I would ask, but I don't want to upset him.

"I can't eat with my favorite person?!" Said Ron while I giggled.

"Of course, but there has to be a reason!" I said. He laughed lowly, while his smile slowly faded away.

We arrived at Denny's. The waitress sat us in the corner booth, our favorite spot to sit. She took our orders and we just sat in silence.

"Are you going to talk to me or are you just going to sit there!" I raised one eyebrow at him.

He ran his hand threw his hair. He looked oddly nervous.

"There are somethings that people can't control. I didn't want to tell you, but at the same time I didn't want to make it worse by not telling you."

He was talking to me calmly. Whatever he was talking about is really making me nervous.

"Rondni what are you going on about!"

I have always had a crush on Rondni. I have this weird pull towards him. I have tried so hard to make it go away, but it won't.

"I'm leaving for a little while." Said Rondni.

"WHAT! Why are you leaving!" I screamed while on the brink of tears.

"I... I am leaving today Valen!"

He's joking! I began to laugh at it like it wasn't real.

" Your real funny you know Ron! That was hysterical!" Tears streamed down my face like a river.

"Valen! I'm serious."

"Serious, because it's mighty funny your leaving me. Let me guess your leaving with some girl that probably doesn't even love you! I care about you more than you think! Why would you leave me!" I got up and ran away.

He never came looking for me. He was already gone. I was young then. So it didn't matter, until I found out why I always loved him.

I felt his hand on my face. I looked up at him. He smiled at me. I couldn't help myself. I wrapped my arms around him."I missed you Ron!"

"I missed you too Valen!"

CHAPTER 4

"Valen!"

My ears rang with my name. I looked up to see the little rascals running towards me. My mom and dad walking from the grand doors of our house.

Ryder and Skylar jumped into my arms.

" Sissy guess what?!" Skylar was practically screaming at me.

"What is it Sky?"

She jumped down and ran to mom and grabbed the big envelope from her hand. I've been applying for colleges around the world. This could be one of them. I want to go the best school. Even though I'm a werewolf I still need money to live.

"Oh my gosh I got a letter!"

I was hesitant to open the letter. The address read Harvard University. One of the best school you could ever go to. It was at least a 2 day trip by plane.

I ripped the envelope open and pulled out a folded piece of paper. I looked at that paper for at least ten minutes. I was extremely nervous and excited. My hands were shaking. I slowly unfolded the letter reading it word for word.

" Dear Valen Dyvenski we would love for you to attend Harvard University to pursue your education of astronomy and astrophysics. Fall semester starts September 10, 2019. Your power is knowledge

Sincerely Harvard University"

I was frozen in my spot. I was accepted to my dream school I'm going to be the first female werewolf astronaut. My mom jumped up and clasps her arms around me. My dad took the letter and screamed She got in!!! Tears of joy were rolling down my face. Everything I want is right in front of me or so I thought.

I was so excited! I started to look for Rondni to tell him the great news, but he wasn't here. I had later went into town looking for him but there was no trace of him. I also stopped by Katy's to tell her the big news.

I finally got back home. I seen him walk in, so I quickly follow in behind him.

"Hey Ron! I've been looking for you. Where you been?"

Rondni continued walking to his room. What is wrong with him?

I got up the next morning and headed to Katy's place. We have some homework to go over even though I know the both of us and we are not going to get anything done.

I walked in and we both went up to her room.

"So what did, you know what, say about that!" I looked at her confused.

"Rondni crazy! What did he say about you getting into Harvard!"

I made an o with my mouth.

"Um... I really don't know I tried to tell him, but he looked tired. So I just left him alone." Knowing good and well he ignored me.

Katy slapped her forehead and shook her head. "You are so dumb Val. He is clearly upset."

"Well he will be okay!" Katy rolled her eyes at me.

I laid down acrossed her bed.

"You know how you felt when he left you all those years ago." Said Katy.

I sighed. "Yes. I do how could i forget. "

"You may not know, but he could have felt bad when he left you. If you left so far off imagine that feeling again, but worse." I listened to Katy.

"Katy when he left he didn't think twice about it. I understand that sometimes you have to leave, but he told me he was leaving the same day he left. He never told me good bye. He never came after me. Yes I was just a kid, but he was still someone I held close to me."

Katy sighed and shook her head at me.

"You may not know the real reason Valen, but this is different now. You know that he is your mate. You are going to want him more badly than you did before. I say just talk to him about it. Okay?"

"Okay.."

We talked and watched some movies. Afterwards i walked home at about 12 at night. A car stopped beside me. For a second i thought someone was trying to kidnap me or kill me. It turned out to be Rondni.

He rolled his window down and asked me "Need a ride?"

"Yea, I need to talk to you." He gave me a confused look after I said that. I walked around to the passenger door and got in his car.

We rode for a few minutes in silence before one of us finally spoke up.

"I"..."You" We said at the same time.

"I'm sorry you go first." I said to Rondni.

"No you said you needed to talk you go."

I took in a deep breath and sighed softly.

"I wanted to tell you that i got into Harvard University for astronomy and astrophysics."

He looked at me with an excited but devastating look on his face. He then patted my shoulder telling me good job.

I could see in his eyes that he really didn't want me to go. That he needed me. I need him.

"I'm proud of you Valen. This is a new step for you. College is where you embrace yourself and figure out how you want your future to go."

He didn't even look at me. He kept his eyes forward on the road.

"I also wanted to ask you how did you feel when you first left. I know you already know that I didn'twant you to leave. I specifically didn't want you to leave me."

Silence was the only thing that was speaking loud. I was starting to grow nervous. I looked out the window to calm myself down, but all I could think about was what is he going to say .

"I... felt like I was going to die without you by my side! I was lost! It took everything for me to wait until you were of age. There were so many times I sat in a chair and just stared at a blank wall for days on end. I just wanted to come back to you! Because I love you Val and I always have and always will! I longed for the day I got to come back to you."

He was crying. Everything was the same for me, until I just gave up. He stopped in the middle of the street. He lifted his head to look at me with those sad eyes. My hands slowly made their way to his cheeks, wiping away the tears.

"Please say you will stay!?"

I looked him in the eyes. This is my dream. I moved my hands. He grabbed my wrist.

"Valen?"

"Ron this has been my dream and it is finally coming true! Can't we just do this together. I want to be with you, but I can't throw my life away. Not now! And I don't have to be an astronaut. I can become an manuel pilot no body has done that before. I'm just spitting out things here. I ... I"

He grabbed my face and kisses me!

"I never said you couldn't follow your dreams! I will follow you anywhere just to be with you Valen. I always will!"

I pull his shirt brining his lips back into me. Longing was in that kiss. Missing each other to wanting each other. We held on to each other not letting our oxygenless lungs stop us. Ron pulls away, both of us breathing heavily. He brushes my hair out of my face. I trace his lips with my thumb. We both laugh.

Ron says "Finally...."

I chime in saying ".....I have been waiting for that for so long."

Chapter 5

I could be the most worst person alive. Ron probably hates me right now. I hate myself. It has been 3 weeks since Rondni kissed me. Being honest I don't regret it, at all. If I wasn't so shy around him I would kiss him a thousand times or more. Nothing he said or did upset me. I now knew what he felt like. I just didn't know how to deal with that, because the whole time he was gone I only thought he didn't feel bad for doing what he did. After I know, my mind doesn't know how to react.

I could feel him lingering at my bedroom door. Pull yourself together Valen. I went to open the door, but I took to long and he left. I'm so stupid!

A small knock came from door. "Valen mama said come down for breakfast!" I laughed as Skylar went skipping down the hallway. I walked down stairs for breakfast. Rondni was sitting there.

I just wanted to be right beside him. "Arrgghhh...!!!" He looked at me. Do something Valen! Fine!

I gestured for him to follow me. I walked around the corner to the laundry room. He followed distantly. He came in, and my body acted before my mind could register. I kissed him! He kissed me back, pushing us back into the wall. This made me think of the first few days he was here. I guess laundry rooms were made for more than laundry. I'm trying to be funny. I'm just not a humorous person.

"I have waited to long for this to happen again!"

"I'm sorry! I was just shocked! I didn't know how to react because I used to "hate" you, but I realized that it was nothing but pushed down feelings that I thought weren't real and...." Rondni placed my hand on his cheek, they looked so natural on his face, and looked me in my eyes."I understand. I thought the same thing the only difference is that you have someone to help. I will always be there for you Valen, I promise." He hugged me tight, I never wanted to let go but we had to.

I ate my food and headed to training. Katy was waiting for me at the entrance."You look happy!" She giggled and twirled her hair. She is hopeless! I waved my hand in front of her face."Katy! EARTH TO KATY!" She squealed and looked at me. "Hey when did you get here?!" Like I said she is hopeless! " I have been standing here for five minutes while you were daydreaming, I'm assuming, a special someone!"

"N..no I'm not, what makes you say that!"I know I'm not the only one who knows she is obviously lying. " It is written all over your face Katy. The giggles and the twirling hair makes it obvious!"

Coach blew the whistle, telling everyone that training is about to begin. We all make our way to the arena." Today, a neighboring pack will be joining us for hand to hand combat training. I will call three people to the stand and you will spar with them until one of you wins!" Everyone was wisphering some were scared others were in-between. The instructors called three names, from the neighboring pack was: Caleb, Nikki, and Hazen. From our pack was : Me, Katy, and Bricen. They picked the three strongest of their trainees. Makes total sense.

"First round is Katy and Nikki! Wolves this is a fair fight! No wolfing out! No biting and or ripping off the flesh. Shake hands, go to your corner of the ring. 3...2...1.. FIGHT!!"

Nikki made the first move almost slashing at Katy's face, but Katy dodged it and side swiped here to the ground. Nikki instantly got back up. She looks very flexible. Katy ran towards her and so did Nikki. Being Katy she never dives in without two different plans. Nikki dives for Katy, but Katy ducks and slashes at Nikki's leg. We all heard

Nikki cry in pain, but she never gave up! Nikki went to lunge for Katy, but failed as her leg was beat up. It was now the last few minutes of the round and hand to hand combat without fancy moves was what they were doing. Katy got a few punches in the he face and gut, but not as many as Nikki did. The timer went off and the match was over. Katy only looked like she ran twenty miles and Nikki looks like she got ran over by an 18- wheeler.

" Katy wins! Next round is Valen and Caleb! No wolfing out! No biting and or ripping off the flesh. Shake hands, go to your corner of the ring. 3...2...1.. FIGHT!!"

I rarely fought with a man, but when I did I wasn't showing any weakness. He slowly stepped towards me. Was he scared?! I mean he looks like he could kill someone and not worry about it, like ever! We were now at least three feet apart. Was he going to try! "Come on Caleb!! For the pack!!" Really they are cheering for him. He took the first swing, I stopped it with my hand. I use this opportunity to jump up on his neck and swing him down. But before I could get him down he throws me off of him. I lie there thinking. I slowly stand up. He is kind of heavily built, he knows I'm quick, and his motive is to keep me down. Ron taught me that everyone has a blind-spot, some can hide it well ,others can not. His is going to take some time. I run full speed like I'm going to jump. Caleb jumps while I slide under him and pull him down. I climbed on his back while he stands up clawing at me. I jump over his shoulders and kick him with both feet right in the gut. I spring myself back up while he holds his stomach. I take a quick look at the timer. I only have ten minutes to win this. He runs toward me looking like he was going to kill me. He lunges for me I roll under him. I immediately get up and run to him to punch him, but I received a punch in the face, and another, and another. I was seeing black dots now.

Valen shift please!No! The rules said no wolfing out!He is obviously wolfing out and no one is stopping him!The rules!I don't care about the rules! Valen as your wolf please just take my word for it!Okay, only halfway.

I let Cecilia take over! He is going to pay! I stopped both of his punches and threw him off of me. I ran over and slash his stomach. I pull him by the head of his hair while he claws at my arm. I sit him up and punch him in the face. I grab him by his shirt and growl loudly at him making everyone bow their heads.

"You broke the rules! Punched me until I almost passed out, over what, that I was pissing you off! You were so caught up on winning you lost the real meaning of doing this. Which is control, self discipline, and responsibility! You and your coach need to reflect on what you just did. Don't come back until you learned all of those!"

The timer rang signaling that the round was over. I really don't care who won. We exited the ring in silence. He didn't deserve a pat on the back.

Chapter 6

I swing the door open and made my way to my living room to sit on the couch. My mom seen my bruised and swollen face. She quickly came and started wiping the blood from my face. Training is the worst and best part of being a werewolf. You come home victorious or beaten up. "Valen who did you fight?!""Someone from the neighboring pack. I'm fine, really mom."

The back door was slammed with a furious Rondni walking my way. My mom jumped up and placed her hands on her hips. She hates it when people slam her doors. Don't ask me why, she just does!"Who is he?! WHO IS THAT MALE WOLF WANNA BE!?!""Rondni there is no reason to be yelling at her. The situation has been handled any ways, right Valen!?" They both looked at me intensely. I handled only a little part. I don't know if my trainer and his trainer even resolved what happened. "I don't know I only said something to him after that I don't know!?" Rondni rubbed his hands on his face, signifying he was frustrated. My mom let out a huge sigh before walking out of the living room. I layed my head on the back of the couch looking at the ceiling trying to come up with some words to spit out of my mouth. Lately my brain doesn't work around Rondni.

"Are you really okay?!"

"Ron I am fine, really! It's just a few scratches nothing more."

"Just a few scratches! Bull shit! He could have put you in the hospital Valen! He could have killed you Valen! He... He!"

"Ron!""He could..""Ron!" "He..could have ki...""ROND NI! He didn't ok ,I'm perfectly fine. See! Look at me! I'm standing in front of you alive and breathing! You know it takes a lot to put me in the hospital."

He walked towards me and placed his hands on my shoulders. His eyes focused on mine. "Valen I don't know what I would do if someone was to hurt you and you weren't there to calm me down."

We both lean in, with our lips only an inch apart before we heard my mom drop something in the kitchen.

We look at each other shocked that we almost kissed each other in the open for everyone in my house to see.

"Valen, Rondni would you both please come help me pick up this glass!"

"Yeah mom! We're coming!"

I sat in my shower letting the hot water consume me. My muscles slowly relaxed as I sat there. What happened at the ring today was bothering me. Not the match, but how I had control over others. I was never able to make others bow their heads in submission. Someone had to be keeping a secret from me. The first person to come to my mind was Rondni.

My family never really asked Rondni where he came from. My pack has shared territory with another pack. Our alpha and the other pack alpha are good friends. Even though both packs live happily together you still don't know who is from what pack. It never came natural to ask since we all basically grew up together. I don't think I know what the other pack is called, because both packs as a whole are called "The Sun and Moon Territory".

A knock on my door disrupted my thinking. "Valen!?"

"Yes Skylar!"

"Mommy said come down for dinner!"

"Okay! Thank you Sky!"

I got out of the shower and got dressed to head down stairs. Suddenly I got a twisted feeling in the bottom of my stomach. There was nothing good about it.

I continued my way down stairs to eat dinner. Everyone was there waiting for me. My face was still bruised, but the swelling went away. Thank the moon goddess I'm a werewolf! My mom had cooked chicken, ribs, ham, and a ceaser salad.

"Mom what's up with all the meat?!"

"You need it to regain your strength and to help with your healing. After every battle every werewolf should eat similar to their true form."

"Let's eat, okay dear!"

As my dad settled us down I felt something intensely starting at me. The hairs on my back stood up. I used my wolf hearing to listen for strange things. Only the silence of the night filled my ears. Something was terrible wrong. I could just feel it.

CHAPTER 7

Legend has told that two packs will join and their name will be many names. Until the two alphas said that their land was called "The Sun and Moon Territory." A jealous pack alpha seeks revenge in the shadows, because he felt betrayed by his twin brother; who joined packs with his friend and not his own blood.

The vengeful brother fought his twin. The other was clueless as to why he was attacking him. The vengeful brother was about to kill when he was informed of his wife and child's sudden death and quickly flead to their sides.

Months passed and everything was perfect until one silver arrow peirced the heart of the twin brother. No one knew who the killer was or how they found the conjoined pack, but wolves believed that the vengeful brother tricked the hunters into killing his twin brother for him. Only the son of the twin could tell the story as they say, but no one knows the son of the twin brother alpha of the conjoined pack, or even if he remembered.

One month has passed and that strange feeling gets strong every day. I steadly hear the voice of my educator constantly wisphering those words in my head night and day. I don't know why? I have no answer, but I still feel that Rondni is the answer to all my questions and can help me demolish these strange things happening to me.

I stepped out of my room and seen Rondni. There was a thick silence as we looked at each other. Around this time of the year Rondni becomes deeply depressed. Someone that meant a lot to him died. Hunters take any chance they get to kill our kind. If it wasn't for the legend of the vengeful brother we wouldn't have this problem. I could feel his heart ache.

I reached out to touch his shoulder, but he walked away from me. His reaction kind of hurt, but feeling only a fraction of his pain helped me understand that he needed some space.

Dad says he didn't see Rondni for months after that person died. He was worried that his friend tried to find the killer, but soon realized that everyone deals with lose differently.

The water felt great as I swam under the waterfall to the hidden cave. To my surprise Rondni was in his wolf form laying on the wet rocks. I should have brought clothes with me, because I was completely naked.His head slowly looked up at me.

"Don't look at me!!" I screamed while throwing rocks at him.

"I'm not looking at you! Please stop throwing rocks at me."

" Are you lying to me Rondni!"

"No, Valen I'm not lying to you look at me my eyes are shut."

I walked over to him to see if his eyes were shut and they were. Then all of a sudden he licks me and I trip and land on my behind. Rondni quickly lays his big heavy head on my lap.

"Ron... Rondni!" I said flustered

"Please let's stay like this! Please Valen!"

"Your lucky I feel sad for you or I wouldn't allow this!"

He let out a huge sigh. Great choice of words Valen you made him feel even worse. I was now mentally banging my head on the cave walls.

I started brushing my fingers through his dark grey fur. When I was little Rondni used to babysit me every now and then while my parents went on dates. One night I was having a nightmare and he came to me trying to stop my cries. He sang me a lullaby his mom used to sing to him before she killed her self.

"Sweet water rushes byYour laughter fills the air so divineI see you in the meadowsSleeping calmly with the sun

Your eyes capture the world around youNothing can make you runaway and hideI'll hold you throughout the daysBecause you are my one and onlyYes you, you are my one only..."

"I can't believe you remember that song."

"It always made me feel better, so I was hoping it would do the same for you."

" Valen do you know who actually died all those years ago on this day?"

" No. I was never told, but I never asked because you were always hurting and I didn't want to upset you more by asking."

" Nothing could make me more upset than I already am, but you seem to make all that disappear when your around me. But today was the day my dad died. He was killed by a silver arrow straight through the heart by a werewolf Hunter."

"Wait... Rondni don't tell me your dad was the...was the twin brother of the legend!"

He picked his head up and walked towards the waterfall.

"Where are you going?"

"I'm leaving!"

"You can't!"

"And why not Valen"

" Because this explains everything I been experiencing for the past month."

"What do you mean 'experiencing'?"

"The day I was fighting at the ring. I growled and every wolf in that arena bowed their heads at me. I keep hearing the legendary story of our conjoined packs in my head every day. I knew it had something to do with you. I just thought you weren't under Alpha Sargent's command and that's why! But no you are the other Alpha!"

"That's my father's past I'm only taking the role of Alpha until my youngest brother can take over! I don't want to live a life looking over my shoulder just to protect those I love! What happened was between my father and his twin brother! No, I have no idea if my uncle was the killer or if it was just a plain ole Hunter collecting his bounty! All I know is that I don't want to hide my family just so that it doesn't happen again!"

Gosh Valen you think you might have pinched a nerve there. I was so caught up in why it was happening to me and the whole time Ron was the victim.

"I'm sorry if I upset you. I just didn't know what was happening to me and I never stopped to think if my theory was right and how this all affected you too. Can you please forgive me?"

He walked towards me and quickly shifted to his human form and hugged me. I didn't care if we were both naked,

I just want him to know that I will always be there for him even if I'm right or wrong." You were forgiven from the start, but next time wear clothes when you have something important to tell me!"

And the moment was ruined.

" Okay that's enough hugging goodbye old man!"

"Hey, get back here young lady!"

CHAPTER 8

Tonight Ron was going to take me on a date. Of course no one else knew except Katy. I'm still to scared to tell my parents. I don't know how they would react if I told them Ron was my mate.

Dad would be like "He's my friend and way to old for you!"

My mother would be like "Rondni how could you do this to my daughter she is only 18! Your using her aren't you!"

And me I'm just gonna sit in the corner and watch my life fall before my eyes. There will no longer be a Valen Issalin Dyvenski, on this planet. No one will remember me!

Anyways, Ron said that his brothers birthday is this week, and tonight was the only night they could celebrate his brothers seventeenth. Everyone is invited. The downside is that the Alpha has to be there and Ron wants me to come and be beside him as his mate and future Luna, which means my parents are going to be there. Thank the goddess that Ron's brother made it a masquerade party.

" Valen what are you going to wear? No, the real question is what are we both going to wear?!"

" I have no clue! Katy please help me.... I don't know what to wear! This is my first official date with him and as his mate/ Luna!"

Did I forget to mention that I also told Katy that Rondni is the dead Alphas son. She was shocked.

" Why not wear red. Classic color, bold, and sexy!"

" This is also why I rarely ask you for clothing advice."

"But you did!" Katy twirled and smiled at me while I was face palming.

We went to five different dress stores. Katy found a dress after the third store, shoes and a mask. I still have nothing!

"Valen!"

" Hey!.....Jeremy?!"

Jeremy is an old friend from school. His family are physicians and human, but they are the only ones we trust.

"Jeremy! It has been so long."

"Yeah I have been at medical school learning to be the greatest doctor the pack has! Is that Katy?!"

"Yeah we are dress shopping!"

"You don't look like you have been."

"Well, I'm still looking for the right dress. The Alpha's brother is having a party and we just decided that we want to go. I'm still looking for a mask to!"

All of a sudden I heard Katy squeal. She immediately came running towards Jeremy.

"Jer Jer! Oh my gosh look at you look'n like a doctor!"

"Yeah! I have been at medical school. Learning to patch you guys up! I have to go my dad needs me. I'll catch up with you guys later!"

"Bye" ....." Bye"

After countless hours of searching I finally found the perfect dress. Me and Katy got dressed at her house. I told my parents that me and Katy were just going to hang out at her place instead.

As we were both finishing our last touches. Someone honked their horn outside. It was Rondni. We both jolted to the front door. Rondni walked to the front door with red and white roses.

"How do I look Katy?!"

"Like a freaking queen! My.. my you look way hotter than me and that says a lot!"

I giggled at Katy's comment.

"Seriously you look like a beautiful and true Luna. I don't care what anyone says, even your parents. You two are absolutely perfect for each other. I will always be there for you Valen!"

Don't cry... Don't cry... OMG Valen don't cry!

"Katy... I don't know what to say."

"Nothing, but a thank you! That's all I ask for."

"Thank you Katy! Your the bestest friend I could ever have!" We hugged each other making sure our little bit of makeup wasn't ruined. Right before Rondni could knock on the door me and Katy opened it.

Ron had on a white button down shirt slightly opened at the top, and a black dress jacket. He had the flowers in his left hand and right hand out for me to grab. This night nothing could go wrong!

Slowly people started to fill the large ballroom. Me and Rondni stood in the balcony. Each person that entered bowed. Ron would respond while I stood there akwardly.

"Relax Valen! No one knows who you are other than me and Katy."

"So much is on my mind, like my parents! Also I'm not use to people bowing to me. Normally I'm the one that is doing the bowing."

"You will get use to it, but not for long!"

Right! Rondni doesn't want to be Alpha!

"Speaking of your parents, look who just walked in."

Both of my parents made their way to us and bowed. I seen my mom wispher something into my dad's ear. They know who I am! I'm dead! Like I said there will no longer be a Valen Issalin Dyvenski!

"I can feel you shaking."

"Who wouldn't be! I just seen my mom wispher something into my dad's ear, and I'm pretty sure it has to do with us!"

Rondni chuckles at me. What is so funny?! I see nothing funny about this situation at all!

"What are you laughing at?!"

"I can guarantee you that they were not wisphering about us."

" I beg to differ!"

"Honestly if you really want to know I could just show you."

Ron grabbed my hand and pulls me towards the staircase that leads down from the balcony. He gently pushes me against the wall and kisses me. Any jitters I had before had completely melted away. I wrap my arms around this neck causing him to step closer to me and deepening the kiss. Then out of literal no where Katy ruins the moment.

"Oo...ok I'm just gonna go!"

"No, it's okay Katy!" I looked at Ron like ' No that was not okay, I was enjoying it!'

"Anyways... Your brother is ready for all of you to walk down the main stairs together. I said what I had to say, so ...um have fun!"

Me and Ron laughed at how quick Katy left.

"Let's not keep the birthday boy waiting!"I smiled and hooked my arm on his.

We meet Damien at the Grand door that lead to the main stairs. I hid behind Rondni as we approached his brother.

"Rondni! Finally your here! I was tired of waiting."

"I'm surprised you didn't already leave us."

"Well I really thought about it and it would be so much cooler to walk down with the Alpha and future Luna."

Rondni pulled me from behind him to fully display his mate to his brother. He quickly snatched my red mask off showing my face.

"Hello...!"

"Valen don't be so shy his family!"

"Sorry I'm still nervous! Anyways I'm Valen and you must be Damien?!"

"Yes, I am! Thank you for coming. If I wouldn't have invited everyone Rondni would have thrown a hissy fit that you weren't here."

I turn around to look at Ron trying to signal his brother to shut up. So he didn't want to be alone! I'm a little upset, but that's so cute!

"Could have just told me from the start Ron! No matter the situation I would have came, yes I wouldn't be as nervous as I am now. What's done is done!"

"Well we better put our masks on! They are about to signal us to walk out." Said Damien while placing his mask on.

I placed my mask on my face. Checking my glistening white dress. Taking Katy's advice was only for the mask. The dress was my whole idea. The red mask made a bold statement and kinda makes me look mysterious ! My white dress was long and drapped from my back stopping right above my back dimple's. A midsized 'V' in the front. My dark brown hair was slightly curled. Tonight I let my hair be completely down.

Then the two grand doors were slowly opening. Ron took the left side of me and Damien took the right.

"Announcing Alpha and future Luna of the silver moon pack and the of course the birthday boy, second leading Alpha Damien."

Slowly making our way down every one bowed and chanted ' long live the Alpha's and Luna!' Ron was right I could get use to it.

The night went on. I avoided my parents as much as possible!! Rondni introduced me to his second and third in command and there son and daughter. The next third was going to be a girl, yes!!

"Well as wonderful as it sounds to stick beside you dad, but I have yet to wish Damien happy birthday."

"Hurry back!"

She sighed and started to walk away. I looked at Mason (aka the third in command).

"If you wouldn't mind Mason I would like to have a chat with Scarlet. To let you and the Alpha catch up on somethings."

Mason nodded and I followed Scarlet.

"Your dad seems rough. Don't get to enjoy being a teenager do you?"

"No offense Luna, but you are older than me and you have already lived your younger years. I greatly appreciate that you bought me some time, but you have no idea what you are talking about!"

"Please set her in her place Valen or I will!"

"I got this don't worry. No one insults our position and power!"

"Actually I do take it offensively, Scarlet. If you were paying close attention to me you would see I am only one year older than you. I nor Rondni said anything about age, but it is quite obvious there is an age gap! If you must know my age then I'm 18 and going to college to major in astronomy and astrophysics! To be the first female wolf to ever study space! Also my problems are bigger than yours so..... please go and do what you wanted, but remember to never cross that line with me again because I only restrained myself this time next time I won't, people or no people!"

" Yes Luna! Sorry Luna!" She bowed and ran as fast as she could. Katy seen me and walked my way.

"I seen you almost bite her head off!"

"That's her problem!"

"What did she do look at Rondni?!"Katy and I laughed at her attempted joke!

"That was not funny at all!"

"But your laughing!"

"Still it wasn't funny. And no she popped off at me after I bought her some time away from her dad."

"Oo...well a lot of people just don't appreciate the sympathy from others."

"Tell me about it! She called me old after I said that her dad was tough and that she probably doesn't get to enjoy being a teenager."

"I'm so glad I wasn't standing there or you would have been breaking up a fight."

" I believe it!!"

We grabbed some drinks and continued to chat near the wall away from the large crowd. We joked about the kiss me and Ron had before she interrupted us. Then out of no where someone tapped my shoulder.

"Hey Valen and Katy!"

~~~~~~~~~~~~~~~~~~~~Hey guys I know it took a little while, but it was totally worth it right?!

I hope so! Next chapter is gonna be a wild one!
~~~~~~~~~~~~~~~~~~~~

LikeShareComment

Love,   Ash_2102

CHAPTER 9

"Hey Valen and Katy!"

We both stood still. Katy slowly turns to see who said our names. So much for masks huh!

"Jer jer?"

"The one and only!"

What!! How did he know? I turned around to see a mask less Jeremy. He was wearing black slacks and a red button down shirt. Jeremy looked handsome, but no one can compare to Rondni. I mean no one!

"Jeremy you can't just walk around and say our names like that!" I whispered yelled.

"Why not everyone is invited?"

" Because Jer jer our parents don't know that we are here. We told them that we weren't going."

"Besides my mom and dad doesn't like me going to another Alpha's house other than my Alpha." I lied

While Katy and Jeremy were still talking I seen my parents walking over to the refreshment table. Where me, Katy, and Jeremy were standing. I panicked and grabbed their hands and dragged them outside to the rose garden under the gazebo.

"What was that for?"

"Yeah what Katy said!"

" My parents were walking towards us so I freaked out and ran out here."

All of a sudden it hit me. Does Jeremy know that I'm the Luna!

"Jeremy how long have you been here?" I question.

" Not long. I had things to do for my dad so I missed the Alpha, the Luna, and the birthday boy. Sucks though I really wanted to see who she was!"

I sighed in relief. I began to become nervous about my parents. What if they knew! What if they knew that Rondni was my mate! What if they knew everything! I was panicking.

Katy placed her hand on mine and mind linked me.

"Are you okay? Do you need some water?"

I nodded my head yes. Katy hugged me and then left to go get me some water.

Jeremy sat there confused as to why Katy left.

"She needed something to drink so she will be right back."

"Oh well, that gives us sometime to talk."

"Talk?"

Jeremy stood up and walked to the edge of the gazebo gazing into night sky. All my nerves washed away as I was trying to figure out why Jeremy was acting weird.

"Valen can I tell you something? Something very important?"

I stood up and walked beside him. I leaned over the edge of the gazebo and looked at him.

"Sure! You can always tell me anything!"

I could hear his heart to begin to race. Jeremy was beyond nervous.

"There's this girl ...who I've liked for sometime now, but she's a werewolf like you. I don't know if I should ask her out or leave her alone, because she might have a mate."

" Jeremy if you like her you need to tell her. If she does have a mate then that would be the first thing she would say to you when you walk up to her. Don't be afraid! You nurse us back to health so this shouldn't be to scary!"

"Thanks Valen!"

Jeremy hugged me tightly. I guess he really needed some advice. Honestly he is very socially awkward.

"So you gonna find her and ask..."

Just before I could finish my sentence Jeremy kisses me! I was in total shock. Right when I was pushing him off he was ripped away from me. Not like I was complaining!

Thank the moon goddess for this hero. Who turns out to be Rondni.

"Val!"

"Ron, Katy!"

"Who is this sick bastard!!"

I look to see Jeremy dangling from Rondni's hand. I was slightly worried that Jeremy was going to die. He is human so...!

"Ron your going to kill him! Put him down now!"

"Not until you tell me why he was kissing you!"

"I don't know the reason to that either! Ask him! He was the one kissing me!"

Rondni threw him down on the concrete and looked at him with his wolf eyes. He was angry, no he was pissed. So this whole time the girl he was talking about was me! How could I be so clueless! I seen Rondni lift his hand to slap Jeremy, but I quickly ran over and stopped him.

"Move your hands!"

"I'm not! If you slap him while you are on the brink of transforming you could kill him! His our future pack doctor. We need him ALIVE!"

"Why keep him alive after he defined me as an Alpha by kissing my Luna!"

"Your... Your what?"

So much for him not knowing!!

"She's my Luna not your kissing dummy!! Why were you kissing her anyways?!"

"Well uh...!"

"He asked me for advice on this girl. I had no idea that he was talking about me. He hugged me, which I thought he was just saying thanks for the advice, and then kissed me. Before I had the chance to push him off you already did that for me so."

He looked at Jeremy like he was ready to kill him, but he walked away. Katy ran to Jeremy while I follow Rondni.

"Ron!"

"Rondni!"

"Rondni stop walking away from me and talk to me please!"

"There is nothing to discuss."

"Like hell there isn't!"

I ran up to him and pushed his chest.

"Stop and listen to me! I'm sorry that you had to see that, but I really had no idea that he would even do that! Jeremy and I have been friends since we were in diapers. I never thought of him in anyway like that, he is like a brother to me!"

Rondni just looked at me in silence. Please say something!! He lifted his hands to my mask and pulled it off. He cupped my face in his hand and I rested my face in it.

"I love you Valen and I know that it wasn't your doing back there, but..."

"But! But what?" I said a little scared.

"I think I need to leave your house for a few weeks and just think for a little while. Not about what just happened, but about our future together. We both want the same thing in life, but at two different times. The elders are getting restless."

"Why are you telling me this now! Rondni you can't do this to me again! I won't allow it....you..you can't leave me again... please don't."

I began to cry. Here we both are repeating history as we try to find a solution to our troubles. Secrets and lies. Future dreams or no dreams. Everything flashed before my eyes. Would we ever be mates again. I couldn't take it.

"You...you can't leave me. I won't let you. I need you Ron.... I..I need you! I love you!"

Katy and Jeremy walked up behind us. I was trying to fight back tears, but they just kept falling. Katy ran up to Ron pulled his shoulder so that he was looking at her

"Hey what did you do to my friend?! Why is she crying?"

He never answered. He just looked at me with a little bit of regret in his eyes. He then shook it off and walked past me and went back in to the party. Katy was about to follow him, but I grabbed her arm firmly. She then looked at me as if saying 'let go' and tried to make me let go.

"I'm not letting go Katy. He just needs to think as so do I."

"Valen.. I had.."

"Don't talk to me! Go home and think about what just happened what you did. Like I said before if the girl has mate she will tell you don't go kissing people."

I picked up my mask and walked home. I never felt so shattered I'm my whole life.

Just when I thought things couldn't get any worse it did.

Chapter 10

It has been weeks since I last talked to Rondni. I haven't been myself since that night either. My whole body aches. Not seeing him, feeling him, and his smell. This is torture. Everywhere I go I just feel like he is there beside me when he isn't. My heart has shattered.

Katy tries to do anything she can to help me, but nothing helps. Jeremy came to my house a few times. Every time I answer the door I slam the door right in his face. Maybe I shouldn't be mad at him, but maybe I should. I regret giving him advice or running to the gazebo and panicking for absolutely no reason at all.

Maybe I am too young for Rondni. Maybe I'm just not good enough. What would life be like if we never meet?

I sat in my window looking out at the foggy mountain tops. The trees flowed down like a stream. The sun barely came over the mountains as the early morning began. Staring into the worlds scenery made me slightly forget my pain. Only for a moment I felt at peace. For that moment my tears stopped running from my eyes. My heart felt like it was never shattered. The aches from my body stopped, but as always it doesn't last long. I went right back into my reality.

I cried and cried and cried until I couldn't keep my eyes open. I feel into a deep sleep.

"Valen... sweetie you need to get up."

"Yeah sister needs to come play with us. Right now!"

"Yeah what Sky said!"

I slowly lifted my head.

"I can't right now guys. I don't feel well!"

Skylar and Ryder looked at me with fury in their eyes. Skylar stepped closer to my bed and began to yell." YES YOU WILL COME AND PLAY WITH US NOW VALEN!!!"

I was already upset and so was my wolf anything makes me lose it and I lost at the most wrong time.

"I SAID I DON'T FEEL WELL NOW LEAVE ME ALONE!!!"

I seen them begin to cry. I felt so bad! I tried to open my mouth to say sorry, but I couldn't open my mouth. I instantly got up and ran out to the mountains.

The wind ran through my fur. I kept running until I found myself infront of Rondni's pack house. Waiting for him to burst through those big oak doors to come and hold me.

Deep down I knew he wasn't here because I couldn't feel his presence. I whimpered in my wolf form. I laid there hoping maybe he will walk by. I sat there for hours. He never showed. Maybe he knew I would come here blindly.

I walk through the front door of my house and see my parents sitting at the table talking to the Beta of my pack.

"What's going on?"

All of their attention lands on me. Two guards walked downstairs with Skylar and Ryder, and suitcases.

"Beta what is wrong!" I asked worried and angry.

He hesitantly spoke to me, " Werewolf hunters are near and we are evacuating all children. Your things are being packed as we speak."

"What about my parents!!" Then it hit me Rondni would have to stay!! "I'm not leaving!!"

"Valen!!" My mom exclaimed"Valen Issalin Dyvenski you will do what you are told!" My dad was furious.

As soon as the guard came down with my luggage the front door swung open. I seen Rondni he had worry all over his face. He looks like he ran for miles to get to me. His wolf eyes still visible. My wolf eyes.

"Valen!" He quickly rushed over to me and hugged me! I embraced him as well. I have missed him so much!!

"What the Hell RONDNI!!" My dad yelled.

"Dad! Chill he is just worried!" I try to lie

"No!! I'm here to protect my mate!" He quickly said after me. I mentally slapped myself.

CHAPTER 11

We all stood there in silence. Rondni protectively stood in front of me. I was nervously standing behind him. My dad was beyond mad, and my mother was shocked. The beta was standing there awkwardly. Why does things happen at the wrong moment.

"What are you talking about Rondni?" My dad said calmly.

"What I just said I'm taking my mate with me to my pack house. My pack needs their Luna!"

Here we go!

"Wait your an Alpha?" My parents question.

The Beta steps and looks at my parents."He is the other packs Alpha. He has kept his identity a secret only I and the Alpha of our pack knows."

"Aren't we trying to get away from the hunters?" I said

"These matters will be discussed later young lady! For now go and stay safe!"

As soon as those words left my dad's mouth Rondni bolted with me in his arms. His eyes still glowing. His wolf might be here, but I can tell Rondni has full control.

I could feel the connection of Rondni's pack trying to force in my head."Don't fight it you need to be connected with us!"

"Ok!" I let the bond connect. I could feel the connection I had with these people. Men, woman, and children. Young or old, I could feel them all all.

I looked up and I seen the pack house up ahead. Pack members were piled around the house awaiting for me and Ron. As soon as we reached the walk way I jumped down and Rondni and I walked towards the front staircase. He was determined to protect me and all the people in his pack. He was tense, but calm. Weary, but strong. A true Alpha looks out for more than just his loved ones, but for everyone in his pack.

Everyone was bowing and saying ' Long live the Alpha and Luna!'I seen scared eyes and worried parents. I seen those who had mates and are soon to be parents hold each other trying to prepare themselves for the worst. This isn't fair to anyone, no one should have to go through this all because a group of people think it's bad that we live even when we make no human contact.

"Rage isn't the answer my love. We must have clear heads. Valen try to understand that it takes sacrifices to protect more in the long run." He said this while looking into my eyes as if he won't ever see them again. He was right rage isn't the answer, understanding and smart decisions are the way to win. I just hate to see so many die.

"Attention everyone!! I just received news that the hunters are 5 miles from the boarder! If you are not a soilder please proceed to your hiding camp's. All soilders report to your defensive sections. Remember our goal is to keep them away from the inner circle of our land!" Rondni's voice was firm and controled. He was confident, but fearful for what might come. Rondni is a true Alpha one of the best you could ever have. With every Alpha there is a Luna ready to fend for her people and loved just as much as he is.

"We got this Rondni!" I said while grasping his hand, which is never easy to let go."Valen I love you more than my next breath if anything happens to you I don't think I could live with myself. Your a strong woman made to be a Luna for any pack. A woman meant to be a loving mother and depent mate. You have changed my life drastically in so many ways and I am grateful for you. I thank you. I am not going to ask you to stay behind even though that is exactly what I want you to do, but being Luna doesn't mean to sit and watch and I know you know that. Follow where your mind and heart takes you." I could see the tears of love and care stream from his eyes. I quickly jumped into his arms and whisper "Not even a silver arrow can stop me from following you and our pack to the ends of this earth. I love you Rondni!"

As soon as those words left my lips he kissed me with passion I have never felt before. Not only does feeling a mate bond make you think you are going to spend the rest of your life with some but the love and true friendship you have with them is how you know!!

~~~~~~~~~~~~~~~~~~~~~~~~~~~~~~~~~~~Hello!! Long waited for update!!! I hope you all enjoy it because the end is coming!! I just want to say thank you for reading my book I had no idea this would blow up like it has!!! I was going to write more chapters, but as the time went on and I wrote more that just didn't happen. I hope you still enjoy it!!
~~~~~~~~~~~~~~~~~~~~~~~~~~~~~~~~~~~

CHAPTER 12

We all Got to the boarder as quickly as we could. Silence was all around. You could hear a leave fall and touch the ground it was that quiet.

Listening for any movement one arrow was shot and then a flood came in. Catching and dodging as many as we can trying to not get hit, distracted by the flood of arrows hunters charged for us. We fleed for the fourth circle of the boarder line looking for clearance away from spiraling silver arrows. We have five boarder lines; the boarder, the fourth circle, the third circle, inner circle, and then the red zone.

A massive amount of howls filled the air following with the pain of losing pack members burn in me feeling their links crumble as if they never existed. Agonizing screams from the hunters as some of them were being slaughtered. I rushed towards any hunter in my sight. I gnashed at their necks watching them bleed to death. I hated fighting, but

I will not stand idlely and watch my people die for just exsiting in this world. There are vengeful wolves out there, but there are innocent ones and we are those, the innocent. I got to area where it was clear from any hunters. I stand there with all my senses at full compacity. Within a mintue I heard these sick bastards speaking about me.

"Someone get me a camera they have a woman fighting out here!"

Three of them all sournding me there are two closer to me.

"Careful man she might want to have a cat fight with you! Hahaha"

One is further back, but not to far.

"As if she isn't worth working up over might as well kill her while we are here."

Imbeciles I can hear you, yet you know that I can, but you think I am useless she-wolf out here.

The two hunters closes to me shoot arrows at me, swiftly reacting I caught them and instantly threw them back, hitting them in their throat killing them instantly. The third took the chance to come down and fight hand and hand.

" I din't think a she-wolf was good at fighting. I thought they were just good for fucking and having children. I guess I was wrong, I suppose."

His words made rage grow from the pits of my stomatch, he wants me to feel this so I don't let any emotion show on my face other than mere smirk to strike fear in him.

" It's quite embarssing that you hunt our kind for living and you have no idea how our society works. It just shows me how inexperienced you are. Killing you will be enjoyable, but a high waste of my time becasue I do have someone I need to being fucking right now!"

His faced was in pure disgust. I could hear how hard he was gritting his teeth from the amount of embarrassment. He began charging towards me with a silver sword in his hands. Coming down on a hard foot I grabbed his shirt dragging hom down to the ground. He quickly stood back up standing his ground. He was definetly not going down without a fight. Which was perfectly fine by me!

" I think it is exciting that you think a mere human like you can win against a were-wolf. Though silver is an effective weapon for our kind it doesn't kill us that fast."

" I didn't ask for your opinion dog! Your kind is an abomination to any race of humans. You filthy creatures kill us and feed on our flesh which gives us the right to kill and make your kind extinct."

" Let me give you a quick history lesson, my pack is not just some random wolves, we are a pack that follow the human laws and our own rule of law. That is respectful towards human kind, that goes for every pack that lives and stands. The wolves that murder all kinds of creatures are rouges and they are vengeful wolves that have gone bizarre. We kill rouge wolves for the saftey of our own and the other innocent lives in this world because they are ruthless animals. Any bit of humanity was swallowed whole. They no longer have the ability to change back into a human after they have became rouge. I just want you to know that you, hunters, are killing innocent people just because you can't accept the difference we have that you don't!"

His face immediatly dropped and his eyes seemed almost frozen in place. He didn't speak a word he just dropped his head and started laughing uncontrolably. He was insane, crazy, phsyco!

" Do you think I care what is murdering innocent people. Your kind deserves to die because you are different and this world won't accept your diffrences. Just like no one in the world would care if I killed you in cold blood. You animals are nothing more than vile creatures who inhabit lands us humans deserve. It's disgusting that a wrench like you thinks a little history lesson could change my perspective on you and your kind. I want to watch you die along with every woman, man, and child. No one will know in any history book that your kind had ever exsisted. "

How could anyone say something so disturbing! He is a rouge human, he has no humanity inside of him. Goddess help his children if he has any and his wife if he has one. If so they live in pain and torture.

" How can you be so inhuman. You are a rouge human and you desreve to die!"

I ran at him full force with everything I had in me. He slashed his sword, but never mangaed to put a single cut on me. I kicked him in the back making him stumble and lose his silver sword. He turned and charged straight for me. Pouncing on his shoulders I lay a few blows to his face to knock him back a bit. He comes back with a round house kick to my neck, but I catch his leg slinging him into a tree knocking any air out of his lungs. Laying helpless gasping for air I push my foot on his throat and watch him struggle with an energy he had left.

" Pitiful to think I wanted to give you a chance to live, but you had to go and ruin that didn't you because now you are a dead man."With that said I snapped his neck and watched his eyes back as he died. His dead face is going to haunt me for a while for sure.

I seen everyone up ahead at our meeting palce. Any living hunters had all retreated signaling their defeat and our glorious victory. I weaved myself through the crowd searching for Rondni. Suddenly I felt to large hands grip me tight from behind, that was my Rondni.

" Rondni!"

" Valen!"

"OMG look at these bruises are you alright do I need to take you to the pack physisian! Come on let me take you to get checked out! Come on Rondni!"

" Valen, Valen baby I am okay stop and look at me. I am right here breathing and standing. My heart is beating, I'm still here I am not going anywhere!"

" Awe Rondni I was so worried!"

I wrap myself around Rondni embracing his touch, smell, and warmth. I don't want to ever lose him not agian. He caressed my head in his huge hands making me feel safe and secure, pulling my tighter into his skin. I found myself falling easy onto him letting my exhaustion engulfed me.

I wake up in Ron's little cottage not far from the pack house with him tangled up next to me in the bed. I roll over to admire this god sleeping next to me. I gently trace his features on his face making them known what this it feels like on my skin. I traced his lips wanting to kiss them and for them to kiss every inch of my body. I want to be mated already with Ron, I want his mark on me, I want all of him. I place a small peck on his shoulder making me excited, but also not wanting to wake him because I want to take in this moment a little longer. I snuggle closer into Ron making him tighten his arms around me. I'm still in awe how this whole time me and Ron were mates even though I had deep down already knew. He is overly confiedent that I am ready to be the luna of his pack and I want to be all that he wants me to be. My dream is standing inbetween us now. If I truly want to go and be the first woman were-wolf astrounaut then that means I have to leave the pack and by duties as a luna down, but if I do this it could possibly weaken the pack even though we are a conjoined pack. With a weak side it can cuase disagreements and a possibly split between both packs leaving the weakest one defensless. I love Ron and I don't want to leave him behind I know that for sure nothing can change that.

Ron opened his eyes and smailed at me. Brushing my hair back out of my face, I could never get used to the spark feeling everytime he touches me. He kisses my forehead making his way down to my lips gently kissing them. I wanted it more rough and passionate so I deepened the kiss forceing my tongue into his mouth. He rolls to his back pulling me onto his lap to feel his erection. His hands start to tease my skin under my shirt making me highly impatient. I bit his lip telling him I want him to take my shirt off and stop teasing me. I seen his eyes change as he roughly pulled my shirt off diplaying my breast to him. He quickly flipped me on my back and started sucking on my nipples between each rough yet passionate kiss. I pull on his hair exposing his neck to let me kiss and suck on his neck giving him enormous hickies. He then pulls my off doing the same only leaving them everywhere. He made his way down to my underwear slipping his hands around them to pull it off of me. He had me fully exposed. He takes my legs and places them on his shoulders while taking in my sweet arousle. Teasingly kissing my inner thighs I let out a small moan slightly arching my head and back in ecstasy.

" Eagar are we Valen." He said in a deep tone. Making my insides set fire even more. before I could catch myself I blurted out " Ron mark me!" He immediately sat up looking at me dead in my eyes. I seen a hint of concern in his eyes. He was worried.

" Valen are you sure you want me to do that? I mean your parents haven't yet approved of our relationship! What about your dream in atronomy won't that difficult to go off and study and not have me there with you everyday?"

" Ron I have thought about it and I am not going...."

" BUT VALEN... THIS WAS YOUR DREAM...." I grabbed his face so that he would look me directly in my eyes and see that I have no regret for my decsion at all.

" It might have been one ogf my dreams, but this being yours has also been a dream of mine for a very long time. I don't want to go through anymore pain between outr relationship anymore. I love you and that is enough for me. I can always find something around here that is similar to what I wanted to do. My only wish and dream now is to be happy with you. I want to wake up in the mornings and admire you while you sleep. I want to feel your skin on mine constantly. I want you to hold me like it is the last time you will see me. I want to be the luna of your pack and the mother of your children. My love for you is greater than any dream I have ever thought of. Your my only hope and dream now!"

He kissed me passionately pulling me close to him. Teasing my oh so eager insides he puts two fingers in makeing me shiver in pleasure and in pain. He enjoyed watching me under his touch. He kissed up and down my body until he found my sweet spot the crook of my neck. Licking it and sucking it he bares his fangs and sinks them into my skin, making me scream out. Slowly the pain turned into pleaure. My body felt heavy and exhausted and Ron looked quite exhausted as well. Releasing his fangs from my skin he kisses sending electricity through my body. He laid his head on my chest and held me tight. I kissed his forehead as he and I drifted back into a deep slumber.

Chapter 13

A month has passed since the war with the hunters invasion and Ron making me his one and only. It's scary to think that I have a great responsibility at a young age to be a luna. Even though I am unsure of what is to come I wouldn't change a thing. I am happy and in love with my Rondni. The pack and my family has approved of Rondni's and my relationship. Nothing will change my mind.

Sitting outside in the grass I could hear for miles. I could hear the wind, all creatures, humans busling in their towns, and my favor was hearing the sound of a water fall.

"Thought I would find you here." Slightly startled by the voice I was still excited to see that was Ron.

"Ron!" Immediately I jump into his arms taking in his warm embrace. His arms wrapped around me tightly while he buried his face in my neck.

"Your so predictable, but I still love you." Placing me down he looked me in my eyes. I could see and feel the true meaning of those words.

"How was everything at the counsel meeting between both packs?"I asked. Ron gave out a loud sigh. There was something bothering him. "What's wrong Rondni?"

"There wasn't a huge problem, it's just that I would like for you to join me in these meetings as my mate and luna of our pack. The counsel agree, but the rules we have set legally you can't join unless I marry you."

"Then why not get married Ron? Are you not ready to be married yet?" Starting to get upset, I was wondering why he thinks that marriage is such a bad idea.

"No ofcourse I am ready to marry you! I just don't want to rush you into anything. I love you with everything in me, but right now you are only familiar with a few things ro be a luna. I don't want to jump into things and cause you a lot of stress."

I could understand where he was coming from, but he isn't putting faith in me.

"Rondni I understand your point, but you can't worry about that forever. We are mates, partners, we burden these responsibilities together! No matter what I will always be there for you. Don't rush yourself into things we have to have faith in each other, okay?"

Taking my hand Ron got down on one knee! I was taking back. I didn't know he was going to do that!

"Valen Issalin Dyvenski will you do me the honor of becoming my wife?!" I began to cry and before I said a word I kissed him passionately. "I take that as a yes then!"

"Absolutely Ron!"

Two days later me and Ron decided to hold a dinner at my parents to inform them on our engagement. Ron was bringing his brother Damien and I had invited Katy.

I glanced at my ring thinking how happy I am to be with this amazing man. We have been through some rough things, but it never stopped us from loving each other. I did find a school that offered astrophysics. I didn't realize I lived near a school with such high-quality. I guess the goddess knew that we needed each other even when our choices are a few years apart.

I place my hand on the door knob to walk in home. I place my ring in my pocket before busting in.

"I'm home!!!!" I shouted for everyone to hear.

The twins cam running downstairs and my parents walked in from the kitchen.

"Valen my sweetheart!" My mom pulled me in close and squeezed me tightly. I repeat the same action as her. My dad walked up and placed his hand on my back. "Welcole home honey!"

"SISSY!!" The twins exclaimed.

I drop down and open my arms wide to embrace these two rascals. Hard to believe I will soon have my own children after me and Rondni get married.

"Sweetheart want to help me in the kitchen while your father takes the twins out?"

"Of course mom."

Mom had almost any possible dish you could think of, well I am over exaggerating. She had steaks cooked with a grand salad and a few side dishes which is roasted fingerling potatoes, steamed broccoli, corn cobs, and fried asparagus. She made sweet potato casserole for our dessert with ice cream on the side.

There was a knock on the door and I immediately knew that it was my Rondni at the door with Damien. Dad had let them in and was greeting them both. Damien made it to the kitchen with small apple pie.

"Damien you know you didn't have to bring anything." I said.

"I told him that, but he thought it would he rude if he didn't bring anything." Said Ron while walking uo beside me and placing his hand on the small of my back. I gave him a naughty look and he responded with a wink.

Later my dear!

I can't wait!!

Not long after Katy made her entrance.

"What 's up second family!!"

We all laugh at her attempt of attention.

"Well then since we are all here why don't we digg in!" My mom stated.We all sat down and did exactly as my mom had said.

"So you two asked to hold a dinner tonight, what do you two have to tell us?" I could see the curiosity in my dad's eyes. Knowing hin he is probably thinking I got knocked up.

I grab my ring snd place it on my hand and Rondni grabs my hand. Clearing his throat Rondni smiles and looks at me.

"Me and Valen are going to get married!"

I place my hand out showing off the ring on my left hand. Katy and my mom start screaming and congratulating me and Ron. My dad was patting Ron on the back and telling us congratulations. The twins were admiring the small, but dazzling ring on my hand.

My mom's curiosity starts to build up in her eyes. "So, when is the date?"

I looked at her and smiled, " We will be getting married in two months, which is May on the third. Tonight I am also letting Katy know she is going to be my maid of honor!" Katy squeals and hugs me tightly.

After the good news was brought up my parents popped open a bottle of wine and we spent the rest of the evening talking about the wedding and looking at my old baby pictures.

Damien left about an hour ago, Katy was picked up by her mate, and the twins were off to bed. I helped my mom clean up and put away the left over food.

"Are you excited Valen?"

"I am, but I am also very nervous. We did plan the wedding quite close and I still have to finish school in the next month. Even though I did give up on going to college Rondni had mention a college not far from here that offers my dream job, but I worried that it could cause issues. I could be overthinking things."

" Oh sweetheart that is only natural. You are stepping into a new chapter of your and Rondni's life. Things aren't always going to be easy, but this is all a sign that you are ready for it all. Your ready for a husband, children, and to be a great luna. You always have me and your father ro help you both anytime never forget that."

Hugging my mother I tell her "Thanks mom! I love you!"

"I love you too Valen!"

We told my parents good night and left my house. We got in the car to head back to our home.. Rondni placed his hand on my leg during the car ride. We reach our home barley waiting for him to park the car we both fleed out the car grabbing each other hungrily. Kissing each other desperately. Slamming the front door Rondni claims my whole body on the livingroom floor. Giving in I wouldn't change it for the world.

CHAPTER 14

As each day passed my excitement and nervousness was growing stronger. With only 2 weeks until the wedding my days became busier with bridal things and luna things, from what color, to following traditions, even down to how quickly will we be having children. As much as I love kids we are in no rush for an heir because Rondni has his brother to take of things if he has to step down temporarily or permanently.

I had waited for this day for years. My Ron and I getting married. Though back then I had no idea any of this was actually possible, but turns out it could and I am loving every second of every moment of it.

"Valen O.M.G you would look so good in this dress!!" Shouted Katy across the bridal shop.

"Katy what did we discuss about you shouting in the store!?" Said my mom in her motherly tone.

"Yeah yeah... but wouldn't you agree that this would look AMAZING on Valen for her reception?!"

"Hey guys what about what I have picked out? You haven't even seen them nor have you seen them on me." I said with a small smirk growing on my face.They both start rushing towards me to push me into the nearest dressing room.

After trying on what felt like a thousand dresses I finally decided on one that would make Rondni drop the reception and take me straight to the bedroom.

Katy, my mom and I walked into the cake shop. Today we were also going to take cake samples home with us today after dress shopping. We all decided to order coffee and blueberry scones for a quick break.

"I think I should do a brunch themed bridal shower!"

"I totally agree! Who doesn't love coffee, muffins and mixed fruit?!" Stated my mom.

"I love anything that doesn't run away from me first!" Said Katy.

We all laugh at Katy's joke and continue to discuss the possibility of my bridal shower theme.

Heading home I was eager to try all these samples with Rondni. Mainly bc I wanted to practice smashing cake in his face. Hehe I'm planning to smash his while head into the cake and of course have one for the guest to have for themselves not the one Rondni's whole head has been in.

Pulling into the drive way I quickly make my way to grab every sample and bust through the door of his study just to sit in his lap like a little girl. Of course he is waiting for me outside. I jump out the car door leaping into Ron's arms. He swings me around and then pulls me into a missingful kiss like he hasn't seen me in months or years. Though I was only gone 3 hours.

"Did you miss me that badly?" I said with smirk on my face definitely giving him that look.

"You have no idea!" Ron replies while his hands move down my body to hoist my body up.

"Oh I bet I do!" I said while wrapping my legs around his waist and him burying his head in my neck.

While walking us both inside making me completely forget about the cake in the car.

As I expected this past week and a few days flew by only leaving 3 days until the wedding. Right now I am in total agony. It's a tradition for our pack that when mates get married they have to spend the last week before the wedding apart. It's supposed to make the wedding day more special because you would be apart and then together at the end.

Katy and my mom have been trying to get me to do anything to distract me from missing Rondni. All I can think about is seeing him waiting for me at the aisle as I walk down to him, living our life long dream. The normal tradition is to have the wedding in the joined pack ballroom . Which is exactly in the heart of the 2 packs, but since I am Rondni's mate and luna we decided that we want to have it at the waterfall. We will have the guest lined through the meadow that gaps between the woodline and the huge lake where the waterfall is. Since it is late summer early fall the bloosms around the rock of the waterfall would be open for our wedding day. Making a gorgeous scenery with little to no preparation.

The reception will be held in the joined pack ballroom. That gives me and Rondni a chance to have time to ourselves after the wedding ceremony. Also for me to have the chance to switch outfits.

"How's the organization going for the reception arrangements?" Said Katy while leaned up againt the study room doorway.

"They are going good! I just can't think of anything else right now my brain hurts from just doing this." I said sliding my hands down my face in frustration.

"Have you eaten anything today?" Asked Katy.

"No I am so stressed out that the smell or thought of food is repulsive!" I said making a digusted face.

"Well you need to eat or your brain won't work properly chick! I'll go make you a sandwich, okay?"

"Okay.... remember no mustard that stuff is disgusting, yuck!!"

"Yes your highness.....hahahaha!" Katy said while bursting into an episode of giggles.

"Ha ha very funny!" I said joining in the giggling episode.

Not long after Katy came back to the studyroom and offered me the sandwich she had made me. Just looking at it had turned my stomach, but I hadn't eaten once today so I need it. I ate half the sandwich and I could feel it already making its way back up. I rushed to the nearest bathroom in my house and threw up every bit of that sandwich. Katy hearing my commotion she ran to me and checked on me.

"Are you okay Valen? What's wrong? Are you sick do I need to het the pack doctor? I'm calling him!!"

Before I could even form a sentence Katy was calling Jeremy our pack doctor.

Not even 10 minutes after she called him he was knocking at my front door painting from being so out of breathe.

"What's.... wr...ong with.... Valen!" Said Jeremy trying to catch his breathe.

"She threw up her sandwich I made her and she said she hasn't eaten because food has been repulsive to her! Do you think it's wedding jitters, stress, morning from not seeing Rondni?" Katy said in a slight panic.

"Katy have you thought they may be she could be pregnant?"

CHAPTER 15

I over heard Jeremy mention that I could be pregnant. So many emotions hit me at once, but before I could even think rationally I step out of the bathroom and say "I'm.... pregnant?!"

"Well I don't know for sure not until I can do test. I brought my medical bag so I just need you to pee in the small paper cup and I dip the test strip in it. It should immediately tell you your results."

Fear was clearly written across my face. I was scared to he a mother I don't believe I am ready to be one yet, but this child is my and Rondni's future so there is no other decision about it. I would believe myself if I was excited as well. This is a new beginning for the both of us and just because we are both in reign we can step down to raise our child together.

I took in a deep breath and grabbed the paper cup from Jeremy's hand. I walk to the bathroom, shutting the door behind me, I take a look at myself in the mirror. I didn't notice that I do look different. Almost like a mother kind of different. I sat down and shakingly held the cup until it was half full.

Pushing myself our the door I handed Jeremy the paper cup. He dipped the test strip in the cup and it immediately turned pink.

"Jeremy what does pink mean?" Katy said with an impatient tone

Jeremy stood there and didn't say a word. He blankly looked at the strip. If I wasn't wrong, I thought I seen a hint of anger on his face as well. I finally spoke up.

"Jeremy! What does pink mean?!"

"It means positive. You are pregnant Valen."

Tears streamed down my face at the news. I was overjoyed, scared, but most of all in love with this unborn child. My own baby to hold and raise forever with Rondni. It also sucks because I can't see him until our wedding to thrill him the big news. I know you are thinking why not mind link him. That is off limits remember the boundaries of the tradition.

"This is so exciting Valen! You are going to be a mother!" Katy exclaimed, overjoyed with excitement.

"I know" I said bursting into a wailing cry.

Jeremy placed his hand on my shoulder. Lifting my face with his as our eyes meet he smiled at me.

"Congratulations Valen! You and Rondni will have a beautiful baby together and I know you both will raise the baby with love." Jeremy nodded then bowed to me as his luna and walked out of my house.

The wedding had finally arrived. I was excited to see my Ron. Our dreams of this day is finally becoming reality. A few more touch ups were being done before I was to walk down the aisle to my future husband.

"Awe... my beautiful Valen! My daughter! You look amazing in your wedding dress baby! I love you so much and I am so proud of you love! I can not wait to see you and Rondni's future together." Said my mom trying to hold back the tears in her eyes.

"Thank you mom and I love you too!" I pulled my mother into a tight hug and slightly nestled myself in her arms like I did when I was just a small pup. My mother is like my best friend to me.

"Luna it is time!"

"Well shall we?" My mother said as I nodded to her in response.

My father waited for me at the door of the tent. He was wearing his only suit (the suit I knew he would wear) he owns. As classic as it is, just the simple backs and white, it suits him. He wiped a tear from his eye and bowed to me as a luna. He then grabbed both of my hands and kissed them.

"You look absolutely beautiful Valen!"

"Thank you daddy! I love you!"

"I love you too!"

We make our way down the aisle and there I see my Ron. My handsome and beautiful Rondni. My now husband and the father to my child. My love of my life. Rondni steps down and takes my father's place on my right side. We see now here at the waterfall infront of the entire pack declaring our love, and bond we have for each.

I do have to say that you look stunning Valen!

You look handsome too Rondni! I have missed you!

As did I!

We were both crying tears of joy at that moment. Starring into each other's eyes like we were the only ones there.

"Together we are here gathered for a special day to be forever remembered by us all! Today we are uniting Rondni Moon and Valen Dyvenski as a one. To be Rondni and Valen Moon. Alpha and Luna of the moon pack and be leaders in the joint pack of Sun and moon. Valen and Rondi do you take each other and pledge to before there for each other in sickness and in health?"

"I do" "I do"

"Do you pledge to be there for each other for better or for worse?"

"I do" "I do"

"Do you pledge to hold, love, and cherish each other even in good or bad?"

"I do" "I do"

"Both of you take the two candles amd light the single candle to signify your unity to for on another. You bonded in your wolf and your human. Your minds will always be at sync. Your hearts will beat the same. Your souls intertwin ed....forever!"

We both took our candles to light the single candle. Our flames became one setting aflame our one candle. Us as a one.

" Now we are going take the rings and exchanges vows! Rondni you may go first."

Rondni took my ring out of his brother's hand. He gently grabbed my left hand a slide the perfectly sized ring on my finger.

" Valen Islin Dyvenski Moon you are my sun and my moon all in one. This day I never thought would come true because I thought how could a young wolf like you could love a messed up old wolf like me. You made me realize a lot of things about being myself and an Alpha of a pack. Though my past haunts me you make it as if it was meant to mean more than just how I see it. Your life means more to me than anything in this world....I love you Valen!"

Tears were streaming down my face. Rondni always amazes me.

"Valen you now may go."

I take Rondni's ring from Katy. I gently grab his hand while gazing in his tear filled eyes. I place the ring on his finger and then begin to state my vows to him.

"Rondni Sawyer Moon. The absolute man of my dreams has became my reality. You have shown me so much love now and ever since I was a child. You bring out the best of myself and I love that from you. No matter what happens we always work through it and never forget our love. You are my entire world..... I love you Rondni Sawyer Moon!"

Rondni was wiping the tears from his eyes as was I.

"I now pronounce you husband and wife! You may kiss the bride!"

Rondni pulls me in and gives me the most passionate kiss. I push myself closer to him and deepen our kiss. We finally catch our breathe pressing our heads together. I bring my hands to his face and take in everything about him. He is mine. My husband. My mate. All mine!

"I love you Valen Moon!"

"I love you too Rondni Moon! Now and....."

Before I could finish my sentence Rondni had collapsed to the ground with a silver arrow pierced in his back.

EPILOGUE

All I could hear at that moment was the cries of the people. My heart immediately dropped. This can't happen! Not now! Not to my Rondni!

"Rondni..... Ron come on wake up please Rondni!! Wake up!! Ron we have to raise our baby together we have to.... you have to to be there!! RON!!" I was screaming as loud as could while I was crying. My eyes were so full of tears everything was blurry. I suddenly felt hands pulling me away from him. I don't want to leave I want to stay with him!

"NO! Please I want to stay with him! Let me...go! I...I don't want to leave him!"

"He's coming Valen, but we must take you to safety."

"Daddy!?"

"I know sweetpea.. I know."

My dad pulled my head into his arms. He picked me up and ran as fast as he could with me in his arms. The guard was surrounding us watching everything, making sure I was to come to no harm.

They immediately rushed Rondni to the pack house medical room. Every door and every inch of the house was guarded. No one except immediate family was able to see Rondni.

I sat next to Rondni holding his hand. The tears never stopped. Jeremy and his father took care of Rondni. They told me thankfully it didn't peirce his heart, but it did hit a vital artery. It can take him a while to recover or not recover at all. He has a 50/50 chance of survival or death. I hold onto the hope that he will stay alive I can feel him fighting, holding to come back.

Jeremy checked on me and the baby. We were both doing great physically, but me mentally I was dying inside.

"Come on Rondni....I know you will make it."

I kissed his hand and laid my head beside him and fell asleep.

A few months had passed. I visited him everyday. I would keep him up with the progress of our baby. Though he was still unconscious I would rub his hand on my belly everyday. So that he would know the progression of our child.

I am 7 months pregnant with our little boy. While Ron is still recovering I had to take up all of his duties. Rondni's brother has been helpful. He is really stepping into his

Alpha genes. Everyday is a constant repeat; handling pack duties, vist Rondni, then go home.

It's difficult watching him lay in that bed for 7 months straight. I can feel him still holding on, but it fades a little everyday. No normal person would feel it.

I walked in Rondni's room. My little boy can feel his father's presence when I enter the room. He jumps in my womb.

"Rondni, our son is definitely a father's boy! He alway knows it's you when I walk in your room! I can't wait for you to meet him. I want you to see him grow like I do everyday even while he is still in the womb. Please wake up soon!"

Tears streamed down my face. I felt to hands rub my shoulders. I thought it was Rondni, but it was only his brother Damien.

"You've grown so much like your brother I almost thought you were him."

"Well he has basically raised me. I came to check in on him. I seen you in here and thought you needed someone to stand with you. I can only imagine how hard this is for you especially when your with child as well."

"It is, but I have you all here with me to help me along the way. You have me to Damien. I'm always here if you ever need someone to talk too."

"Thank you Valen. How about I take you to Dennys like Ron did with you sometimes?"

"That would be great."

Another 2 months has passed. I am due any day now. Jeremy has been keeping an eye on me constantly. So has my mom, dad ,Katy , Damien. They are all excited and worried for me.

I sat in my little boys room rocking back and forth looking out the window. I can smell the early summer breezes with a mix of late blooming flowers as I watch the wind sweep through the forest. I can feel the warmth of the sun on my skin as a think about all the days at the lake. The ones alone and the ones with Rondni.

Knock knock

"Come in."

"Valen. "

"Jeremy."

"I came to check in on you. Any pains?"

"Just a few Braxton hicks. Nothing that is letting me know that the baby is coming. Any progress on Rondni?"

"He is recovering. I believe he will be awake within a few weeks. I'm sorry he won't be there for the birth of y'alls child."

"It's quite alright. I'm just glad he is getting better. I can finally feel him at almost complete health."

"Your baby's nursery looks amazing. I had no idea it was finished."

"Thank you Jeremy. I had Damien help me finish most of it."

"Damien has been a great help for you these past 9 months."

"Yes he is doing great as an Alpha right now and he is being an amazing uncle to his unborn nephew. He is an even more of an amazing brother-in-law to have around. I honestly I have no idea what I would have down if he didn't step in and help me. I own him a great deal of gratitude for all of his help."

"I'm glad."

I stood up and walked towards Jeremy, but when I stopped in front of him my water broke. "Did ... my water just break?"

"I do believe so!"

"Jeremy call everyone. I'll meet you at the birthroom."

"Can you make it there by yourself?"

"Are you really asking me that right now?!"

"OK sorry I'll call everyone!"

I make my way to the birthroom in the house. It took me a little bit trying to walk inbetween contractions.

Everything was happenimg so quickly. I was already dilated 8 centimeters. Each contractions getting closer and more painful each time.

"OK valen push!!!"

I put every ounce of my energy to push as hard as I can.

"Doctor!!"

"Yes what's wrong?! If it is not important then it can wait until after I help Valen deliver her baby!"

"It's the Alpha sir he has been poisoned!"

"Wh..at.... what do....you mean... argh... poisoned?!" I saidAll of my energy being put into giving birth I didn't feel Rondni in pain. I was searching and final found a faint heart beat. RONDNI PLEASE DON'T GO STAY FOR ME AND TOUR CHILD!!!

"I am coming!!! Jeremy deliver the baby! Now!" After that said the doctor fled the room leaving the rest of us praying he will be alive!

" Okay Valen I can see the crown of the babies head one big push and the baby will be here ok!" Said Jeremy with a shaky tone in his voice.

I grit my teeth and push and push. Suddenly I felt a huge emptiness in my chest.

"NO...... RONDNI!!"

He was gone...

Each time I could feel the electric shock raging through my body everytime they tried to shock Rondni's heart back to life. No response no heart beat no link holding me and him together anymore.

In the background I hear a baby walling. I open my eyes to see my baby boy's face. He looked just like Rondni.

"My... my baby boy!" Tears were streaming down my face. I reached out and held my precious baby boy. His crying stopped as soon as I laid my hands on him.

"You look.... you look just like your father. You are our precious boy.... my whole world revolves around you my son!"

"Valen... I just got word...." Jeremy was saying before I cut him off.

"I know Jeremy .... I know. I can only remember Rondni from the memories and see him clearly in our son, but it is okay because I have something to live for. My reason of living is for the child me and my Ron have made out of our own love for each other now and forever! His name will be Rhys Rondni Hart Moon!! My sweet baby boy!"